T0380323

The Adventures of Abby and the Seahorse

Go to Texas

B.I PHILLIPS

To order additional copies of this book, contact:
Xlibris
844-714-8691
www.Xlibris.com
Orders@Xlibris.com

ISBN: Softcover   978-1-6641-6535-9
       EBook   978-1-6641-6534-2

Print information available on the last page

Rev. date: 04/23/2021

Abby and seahorse leave Tampa
Text : Let's go to Texas

Abby and seahorse encounter
floating mushroom . Which
the mushroom says

"Help me, Help me their is
a hurricaine coming ."

Abby said, "they said their wasn't."

Fish says "Welcome to the
Flower Garden Reef."

"This is the Stetson bank."

some of the fish are endangered.

"Bring them back"

"oh no our boat is gone ."

Green Whale said, "I can
bring you home."

"Thank you. Let's go"

"Oh no the hurricane! "

Green whale, "no worries
we can go under it."

Thank you green whale
for the ride home.

Printed in the United States
by Baker & Taylor Publisher Services